THE BIG STINK

Lucy Freegard

PAVILION

Meet Charlie.

Charlie **loved** cheese.
A bit too much perhaps.

Some might say he had an
unhealthy obsession.

He read about cheese,
dreamed about cheese,

and watched cheese
videos on his computer.

Charlie didn't have much money. He knew that stealing wa
wrong, but sometimes his cravings were just too strong.

He pinched Parmesan,

crept
off with
Camembert,

and robbed Roquefort.

But now, Charlie had bigger plans.

Every day, at the Museum of Cheese, people would queue up to see The Stinker – a famous (and delicious) work of art.

Mona Cheesa
Leornardo da Stinky

MUS

And every night Charlie would dream about breaking

UM OF CHEESE

The Stinker
Auguste Rodent

Cheese of Man
Rene Margherita

OPENING TIMES

PLEASE
WAIT
HERE

into the museum and stealing The Stinker for himself.

Then one night...

...Charlie sat...

...and he waited...

...and he waited
some more...

... until the coast
was clear.

Quiet as a mouse, he climbed up to the very top of his ladder and broke in through an open window.

Charlie crept past
every gate,

every camera...
...and every guard.

He tiptoed down the corridor until he reached the last room.

Charlie took a deep breath and prised open the door.

NO ENTRY

He had broken into the wrong room!

Or had he?

Charlie cut a hole in the floor…

...and carefully lowered himself down to cut The Stinker out of its case.

Mona Cheesa

The Stinker

One by one Charlie crawled under…

… and climbed over the lasers.

He was very careful not to touch a beam,

because that would be a complete…

...DISASTER!

"Uh oh!"

"Someone's stealing The Stinker!"
said the guard into his radio.

"Quick, send back-up! And a nose clip!"

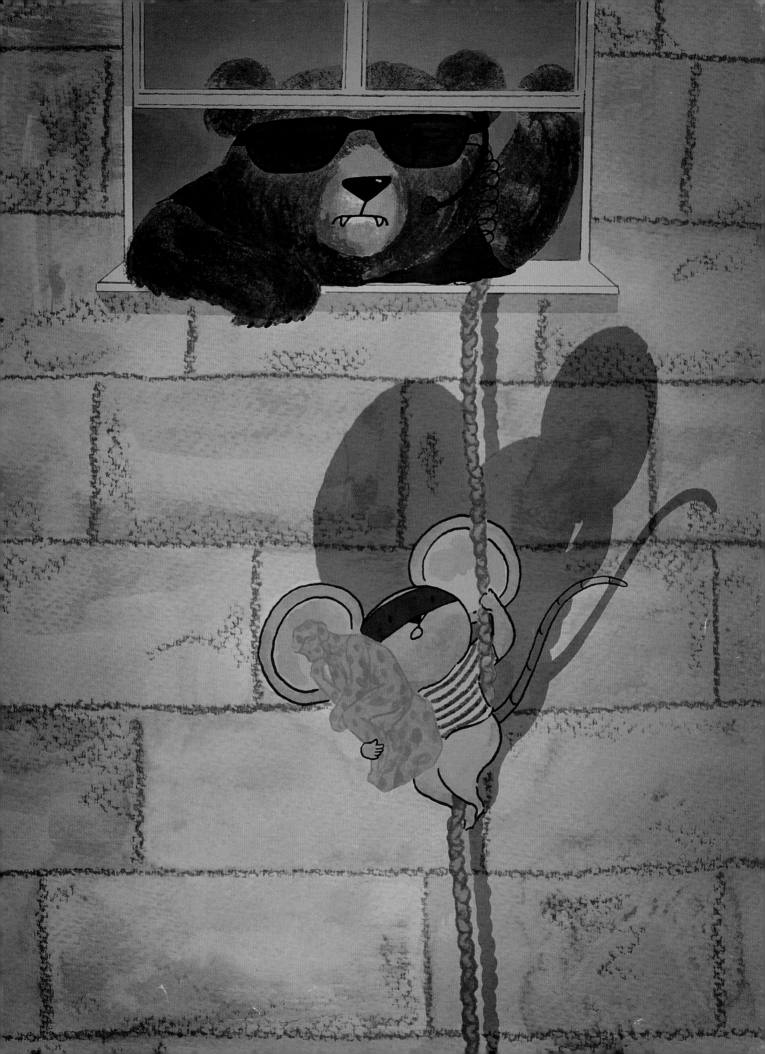

"You can't run forever," called the cops.

But Charlie was a mouse on a mission.

CRIME SCENE DO NOT CROSS CRIME SCENE D
DO NOT CROSS CRIME SCENE DO NOT CROSS
1

The mischievous mouse
disappeared into the night.

But Cheesetown put their top
detective on the case – Officer Rita.

DO NOT CROSS CRIME SCENE DO NOT CR

CENE

T CROSS CRIME SCENE DO NOT CROSS CRIME

With the help of her team, Officer Rita
collected clues and examined the evidence.

And then finally, fuelled by a strong suspicion,

and a super sense of smell,

Officer Rita traced Charlie

all the way to...

...his secret hideout!

Luckily for the Museum of Cheese, Charlie had decided that the sculpture was too beautiful to eat.

But he had still taken his love of cheese a bit too far.

While paying the price
for his cheesy crime,

Charlie had lots of
time to think.

That was when he
had his great idea.

The Stinker had inspired him to become a cheese sculptor!

He crafted wonderful works of art... and could eat all the crumbs too!